For Laurel and Josh, wishing you
a lifetime of happiness together.
—K.D.

For Emily, James, David, and Daniel.
—M.K.

RODALE KiDS

An imprint of Rodale Books, 733 Third Avenue, New York, NY 10017
Visit us online at RodaleKids.com.

Text © 2018 by Kelly DiPucchio • Illustrations © 2018 Rodale Inc.

Rodale Kids books may be purchased for business or promotional use or for special sales. For information, please e-mail: RodaleKids@Rodale.com.

Printed in China. Manufactured by RRD Asia 201803.

Design by Eric Wight & Jeff Shake

Library of Congress Cataloging-in-Publication Data is on-file with the publisher.
ISBN 978-1-63565-140-9 hardcover
Distributed to the trade by Macmillan
10 9 8 7 6 5 4 3 2 1 hardcover

HOW TO GROW
HAPPINESS

A JEROME THE GNOME ADVENTURE

KELLY DiPUCCHIO

PICTURES BY **MATT KAUFENBERG**

RODALE
KiDS

W

arble flew through the Garden of Wonder into Jerome's open window. "I brought you something special today," she chirped.

CHIRP!
CHIRP!
CHIRP!

Jerome examined the tiny black seed resting on the window ledge.

"What kind of seed is that?" asked the curious inventor.

Warble smiled proudly. "It's a seed of happiness!" she declared.

Jerome, being a collector of treasures and trinkets, was very interested.

He reached for a glass jar on the shelf and emptied the contents into his hand.

"I will trade you this bit of red yarn for that seed," he said to his small friend.

Warble looked pleased. "That yarn will be perfect for my spring nest," she sang. "Thank you!" She scooped up her new treasure and flew away.

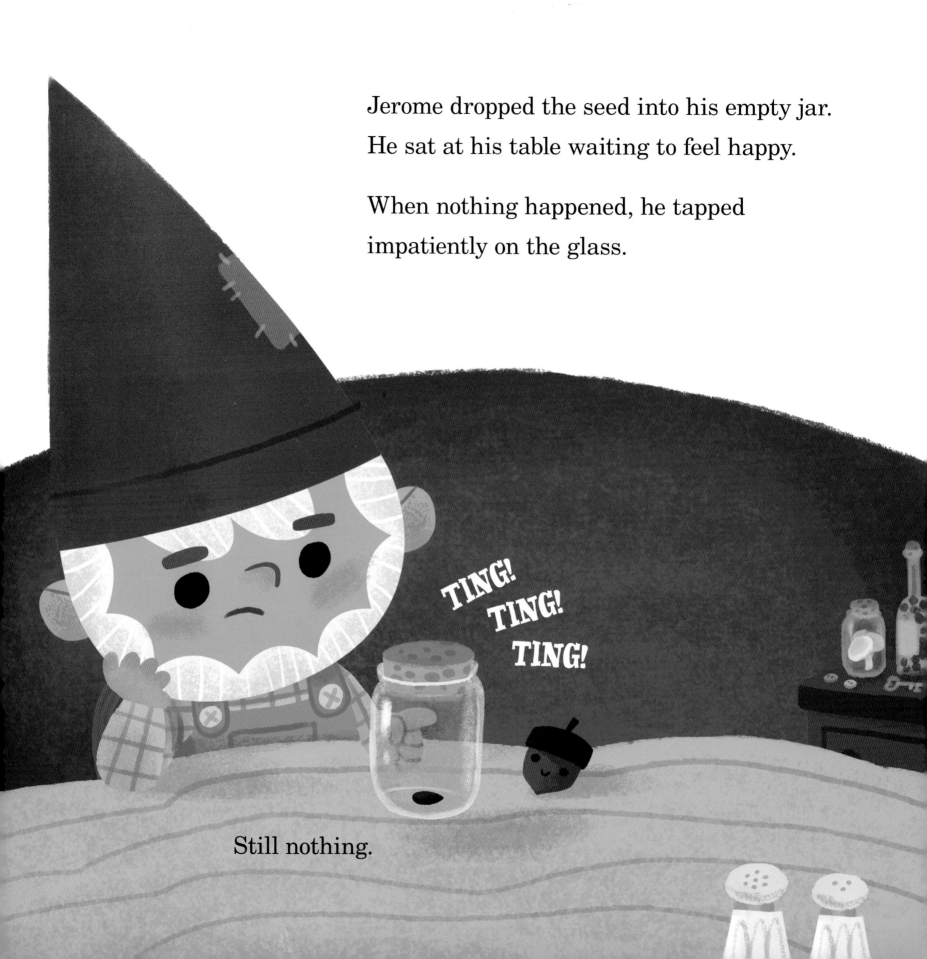

Jerome dropped the seed into his empty jar.
He sat at his table waiting to feel happy.

When nothing happened, he tapped
impatiently on the glass.

TING!
TING!
TING!

Still nothing.

Jerome became frustrated and shook the jar. The tiny seed bounced up and down, but Jerome didn't feel a hint of happiness.

He turned to Oakie, his pet acorn. "I think Warble gave me a broken seed," he grumbled.

"A broken seed? Where?" asked Nutilda as she burst through the front door. Beamer, the robot, followed close behind.

Jerome showed his jar with the seed inside to his friends. "It's not broken," insisted Beamer. He pointed to his solar panel. "It just needs a little sun to work. Like me!" "He could be right," said the squirrel.

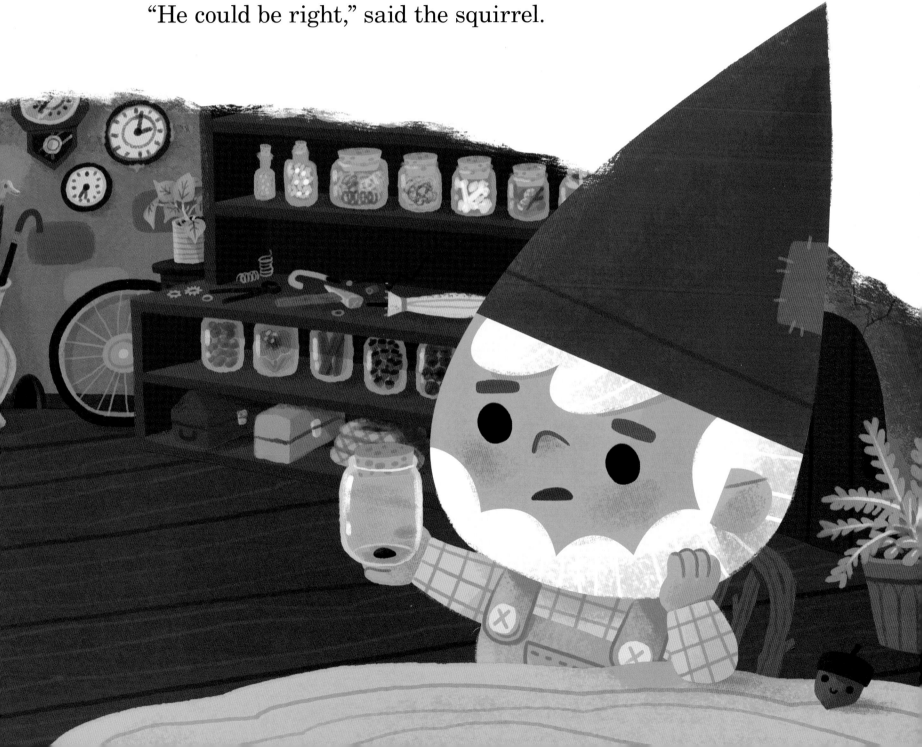

Jerome agreed. He took his jar outside, placed the seed on a rock in the hot sun, and counted to 10. He sighed loudly. "I'm still not feeling happy."

"Neither am I!" snapped Sir Surly. "You woke me up from my nap. And that seed of yours is getting too hot! It needs water!"

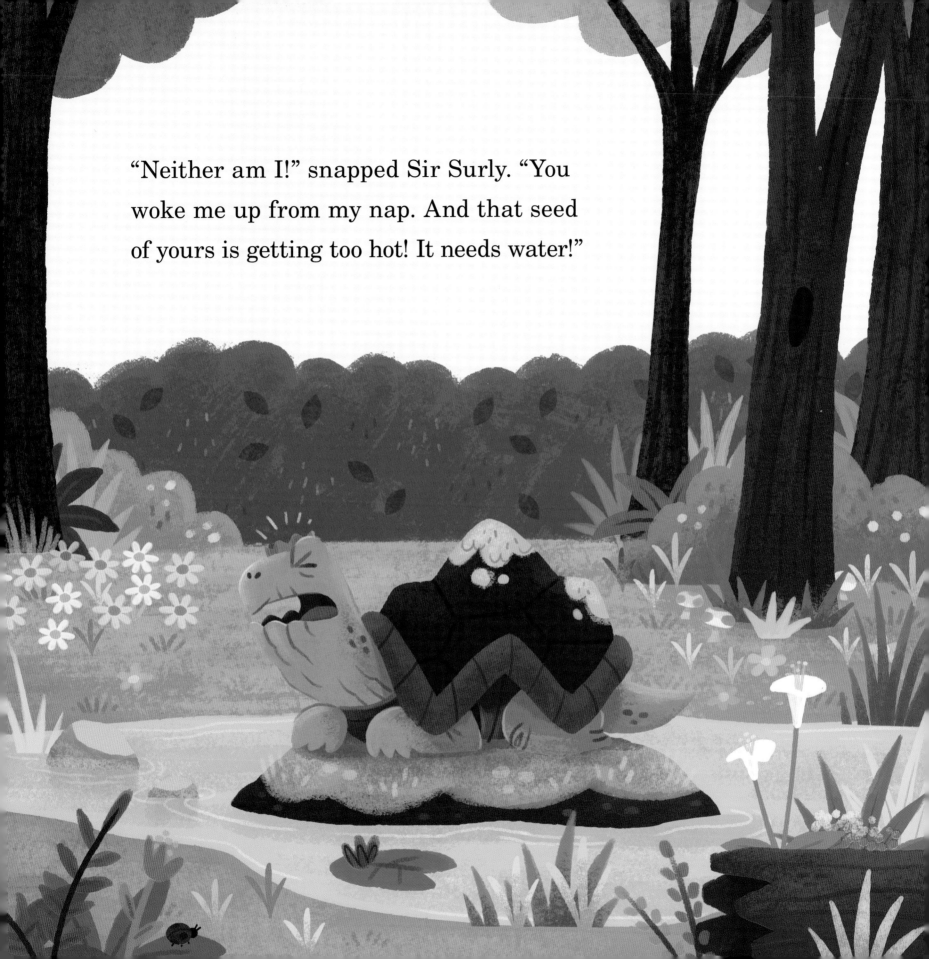

"Of course," Jerome said to the turtle. "Why didn't I think of that?"

He tossed the seed into the pond.

"Good heavens!" cried Sherwin Wigglesworth, inching
his way toward the shore. "Not that much water!"

The worm climbed up on the rock. "I know a thing or two about gardening!" he boasted. "Your seed needs dirt. But not just any dirt—dirt with egg shells, coffee grounds, and banana peels."

Jerome smirked. "Who knew a little seed could eat so much?"
He fished the seed out of the pond, then covered it with dirt
and his morning trash.

Aroma joined the circle of friends. "What is everyone looking at?" she asked.

"Warble gave Jerome a broken seed of happiness and we're trying to fix it," Nutilda explained to the skunk.

"We've tried sun," said Beamer.

"And water," said Sir Surly.

"And dirt," said Sherwin.

"But I still don't feel very happy," Jerome complained. "As a matter of fact, I'm feeling angry with Warble for taking my red yarn and giving me a worthless seed."

"Oh dear," whimpered Aroma, accidently spraying her scent.
Aroma didn't care for unpleasant situations.

They made her nervous.

Glinda, the butterfly fairy, fluttered over to the troubled group. "You all forgot something important!" she chimed in.

"What's that?" asked Jerome, feeling more discouraged than ever.

"Love! The best things always grow from love,"
she said, disappearing over the bramble bush.

Jerome thought about what Glinda said. He suddenly felt compassion for the tiny, helpless seed, who must be feeling lonely buried beneath the heap of dirt and trash.

"I'll be right back," he told his friends.

Jerome returned with a jar filled with his favorite stones.

He placed the stones around his makeshift garden.

"There." Jerome smiled.

"I must admit, I'm feeling a teensy bit happy."

Jerome tended to his seed every day, making sure it got just the right amount of sun,

water,

food,

and love.

He watched a short green sprout grow into a long green vine.

As the vine grew,
his happiness grew and

and

grew

until one day . . .

"FRIENDS!"

Jerome called out cheerfully.

"Come quickly!"

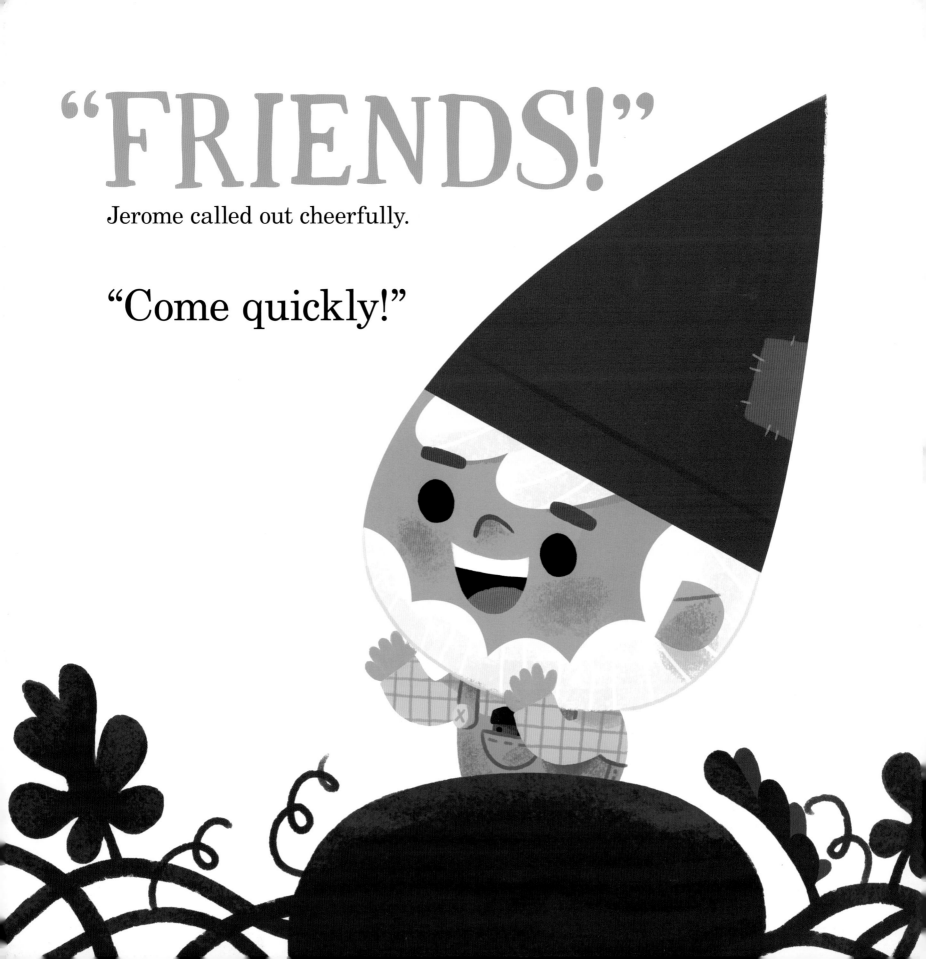

Jerome's friends gathered around him.

"Look!" he exclaimed, pointing to his garden.

The tiny black seed had grown into
GIANT green watermelons!

"I'm sorry I ever doubted you,"
Jerome apologized to Warble.

"It's okay," said the bird. "Sometimes growing happiness
takes a little hard work and patience."

"And sun!"

"And water!"

"And dirt!"

"And love! Don't forget the love!"

The friends laughed and enjoyed a summer picnic in the Garden of Wonder. They each went home that day with their own seeds of happiness.